Domination

Chase H Auburn

Copyright © 2025 Chase N Auburn.

All rights reserved. No part of this book may be reproduced, stored, or transmitted by any means—whether auditory, graphic, mechanical, or electronic—without written permission of both publisher and author, except in the case of brief excerpts used in critical articles and reviews. Unauthorized reproduction of any part of this work is illegal and is punishable by law.

ISBN: 979-8-89419-758-6 (sc)
ISBN: 979-8-89419-759-3 (hc)
ISBN: 979-8-89419-760-9 (e)

Because of the dynamic nature of the Internet, any web addresses or links contained in this book may have changed since publication and may no longer be valid. The views expressed in this work are solely those of the author and do not necessarily reflect the views of the publisher, and the publisher hereby disclaims any responsibility for them.

One Galleria Blvd., Suite 1900, Metairie, LA 70001
(504) 702-6708

DEDICATION

I would like to thank my husband, Master & friend, Robbie for without his emotional, & financial support this book would not have been made possible. He helped achieve a life long dream.

To my sweetest friend, & favorite fan Gene.. who has been behind me since the first publication of DOMINATION, had I never gotten published, I would never have had the honor of having him bless my life.

To all that have supported my endeavor... Thank you.

DOMINATION

Opening the door to the two – story home, things don't "feel" right. A cold hand races up the back of Damon's spine, setting the hair on the back of his neck and to stand on end. Closing the wooden entry door softly behind him, Damon glances around the foyer for any signs of disarray.

Setting his briefcase onto the floor next to the wooden seating bench, he lets his duffle bag slip off his shoulder to the flat surface of the hand carved wooden seat. Taking a wary step into the open greeting space between the staircase and the den, he hears the soft melody of soft rock playing low over the in-house speaker system.

Stepping silently into the archway of the front sitting room, he moves silently through the still room, his instincts kicking in instantly as he slips toward his left to peer into the silent den. Noting instantly that Leigha's laptop is resting untouched on the padded seat of her favorite wing-back chair. Narrowing his eyes, the thought races through his mind that perhaps, she's not within the confines of the walls of the house at the moment. Unusual for his kajira however, since she doesn't care to be out and about without his presence at her side.

Stealthily moving past the door frame of the den, Damon moves with military-trained precision through the short hall to the elegant dining room. Slipping into the room, his eyes adjust to the bright sunlight streaming through the cut glass windows, windows Leigha insisted on having installed when remodeling this particular room, she argued that the diamond cut of the glass gave the room a feel of true renaissance elegance to contribute to her role as his kajira, or slave, within the lifestyle.

Moving with a cat-like grace, Damon enters the doorway leading into the kitchen. A sudden fear grips his core as he again sees no sign of his jewel, stepping into the kitchen he walks to the small window nook where a table sits in the afternoon sunlight. Yet more windows, he understood her need for light, after the abusive relationship he seemingly rescued her from, he never once condemned her request to add larger windows into the home as the remodeling was being completed.

The darkness was something she could not contend with, her captivity in the darkened chamber could not be overcome. It was the one fear she still carried with her, even after coming to him six years ago. At the age of twenty, Leigha had seen enough abuse from her former master to last two lifetimes. Stepping to the table, Damon searches its empty wooden starburst-designed top for some sign, a note, something telling him where she may have disappeared to.

Turning in a complete circle, his eyes scour the countertops to no avail. Cursing under his breath, he moves with speed and urgency back through the dining room, into the hall, and into the open sitting room. Glancing again into the den, he moves with trained grace toward the wooden staircase, noticing with a slight furrow to his brow that the wood appears to have been freshly polished, meaning, Leigha couldn't have been gone long before his arrival.

Reaching out to touch the ornately carved wooden dragon adorning the staircases' banister, Damon halts with hand in mid-air as he glances again towards the den. Letting his hand drop to his side from the carved dragons' head he steps into the plush carpeted room.

Chastising himself silently for having worn his shoes onto the cream-colored carpet, any marks and he will have to be the one to clean the plush fiber in the barefoot only zone.

Moving across the eerily silent room, he steps into the rays of sunlight streaming through the stained-glass windows. Another feature Leigha had to have, looking up into the diamond-cut glass, his eyes fixed on the white winged stallion. The image portrayed in the cut glass is of a mighty steed flying across the blue skies beyond the confining glass of the window. Wings proudly spread with strong delicate legs stretching into the heavens. Atop the stallion sits a slim, petite figure wearing an emerald gown, the material of the deep green gown flows across the stallions' rib cage, just under the outstretched wing of the Pegasus. Her long auburn tresses flowing freely in the wind behind her silhouette catches the rays of the sun streaming through it's shimmering length.

His Leigha, *His* jewel. That particular pane of glass was custom designed to depict the woman that stood out above all the others. The one woman, he could not turn from. Cannot resist. His Leigha, *HIS* Jewel. Tearing his eyes away from the picture window, Damon steps apprehensively closer to the chair, the pretty wing back chair she enjoys sitting in while writing provocative stories for his amusement while he is away on business trips, which always seem to tear him from her side.

Stopping in front of the chair, he leans over slightly, reaching long fingers towards the computer, a thought stops him in his tracks, and straightening his spine, Damon slowly looks around the room, taking in every small aspect of the silent room. Everything in the home was being remodeled to imitate the look and feel of a renaissance era castle, even the fireplace adorning the interior corner of the den, with its intricately carved mantelpiece of broad wood, depicting the image of two dragons soaring above the mountaintops. Above the mantel, a wooden depiction hangs of carved dragons with wings open, the mighty beasts seem intertwined in a lover's embrace.

Looking upon the carving Damon feels a twinge of fear in his chest, as he gazes upon the intricately carved visage. The dragon's talons are interlocked As those in a lovers embrace fingers, breasts touching slightly as the great beasts rise as one with tails twisted into a point.

The creation again causes the feeling of dismay to wash over Damon as he recalls the night, he, and Jewel ordered the hand carved artwork from a craftsman at one of the renaissance fairs they had attended. Having begun to lose hope in ever finding someone that could carve the picture exactly how it looked in the image Leigha had found on the internet; he remembered her excitement when coming across the woodcarvers' stall.

Forcing his gaze away from the carving, he tentatively lifts the lid on Leigha's laptop, hoping to find a note, either on the screen or printed between the computer's lid and keyboard. Finding nothing, Damon draws in a steadying breath and closes the lid on the laptop, leaving the computer as he found it.

Moving towards the staircase, he glances once more around the room. Hoping to see something he may have missed. Seeing nothing, Damon leaves the room and heads to the mahogany staircase.

Placing a foot against the first step, he halts as he thinks he's caught a slightly muffled sound coming from somewhere within the house. Hearing nothing more, his hand rests lightly on the wooden banister as he ascends to the upper level of the home.

Moving with the speed and grace of a well-oiled military machine, Damon moves into the first room to the right at the top of the stairs. Noting everything seems to be in place, he purposely walks into the room and throws open the storage closet door. Taking a quick inventory of the contents, he's relieved to find the suitcases on the top shelf above the hanging coats untouched.

Shutting the door, he moves around the small room with care, checking the window sills for any signs of damage. Thinking perhaps someone had entered the home in this manner, undetected in his absence. Seeing nothing amiss, Damon moves back into the hall running the length of the upper floor.

Moving with catlike grace down the hall a few steps, Damon stalks to the next closed door. Listening for a brief second, he turns the knob to allow himself into the suite of his slave. Normally, he wouldn't permit himself to rudely barge into the room without first knocking, but a sick feeling in the pit of his stomach urges him onward. Opening the door, he finds the queen size bed made properly in its vibrant golden comforter, her embroidered pillow shams gracing the pillows at the head of the bed, a light cream-colored lap quilt folded neatly across the foot of the silk cover, to the left of the headboard, her journal sits quietly on the nightstand under the twisted iron table lamp.

Walking to the side of the bed, he lifts the journal from its resting place and turns it over in his palm, the green velvet cover, soft under his fingertips, replacing the treasured book, unopened, Damon glances to the matching side table to the right of her headboard. The matching lamp sitting proudly in place on the hand embroidered stand doilies, lovingly made while Leigha had taken such pains to finish while he had her trapped in a hotel while on one of his business trips.

The original plan had been to take her site seeing in the beautiful Venetian valley, however, between the rains that had set in and Leigha becoming ill, to the point a doctor had to be called, having discussed her condition, the best course of action was to keep her in the safe comforts of the suite while he conducted business. Her view had been breathtaking at least and aided in the consolation of not being able to go out and about. Promising her another trip, at a later date, make her quite content to have a local woman show her the basics of hand embroidery, from there, the needles seemed to have a life of their own in her delicate fingers.

Seeing nothing to alarm him to foul play, Damon leaves the room as untouched as possible, carefully latching the door at his exit, he again listens to the quiet of the house as he moves down the hall, sticking his head into the quest suite directly across the hall from Leigha's door, he finds nothing to show that perhaps a visitor had popped in unannounced and stole Leigha away for a luncheon.

Leigha was under the impression he would be gone a few extra days on this trip, the meeting didn't go according to plan, so Damon removed himself until minor details and negotiations could be worked out.

Shutting the guest room door with a quick pull, he stares at the door immediately to his right leading to the hall bathroom. Not having heard any sounds, he decides it's still best to investigate the room. Grabbing hold of the door handle, he slowly pushes the door open, the room is silent and still, nothing out of place, towels hanging folded as should be, and the tub appears not to have been used recently, shaking his head, Damon moves back into the hall.

Turning his attention to his right, he's left standing dead center of the end of the hallway, facing the only room remaining, the dark ornate mahogany doors leading to the "Master's" suite. His private chambers, at least until he managed to finally convince Leigha to move in with him. She still enjoys her quiet time in her private room at times, however. She tends to sleep there when he's away at length on trips also, taking a deep breath and saying a small prayer, Damon opens the massive door to find and silent and empty room.

Cursing softly, he enters the room. The faint scent of her perfume lingers in the enclosed space, standing silently, Damon breaths deeply of the intoxicating aroma of her perfume. Memories flood his senses, shaking his head to free himself of the invasive bodily reactions of the memories flooding him, he walks to stand before the massive king-size bed centered in the middle of the room, and he seeing everything as it should be. Everything is in place from the deep emerald green silk comforter, to more of Leigha's embroidered pillow shams and dresser doilies with matching dresser scarves.

Nothing out of sorts. Her black satin, full length robe hangs seductively over the back of an antique dressing chair she found at one of the local antique dealers in the area. The matching satin ballet slippers sit just under the chair, peeking out by the toes as if playing a game of hide and seek.

Running a frustrated hand through his thick hair, Damon moves across the room to face the double frosted glass doors of his study, opening the doors, he finds his desk the way he left it a few days ago. Walking to stand in front of the silent computer, he rummages about his desk looking for a note, ribbon, silk binding, *anything,* that would give him the slightest clue as to where his slut has gotten to.

The feeling of doom begins to slowly creep into the back of his mind, trying to stamp it down, his mind wanders back to a previous conversation they had before he left this last time. He had thought Leigha was being paranoid when she kept telling him that her former owner wouldn't allow her to go easily. The one Damon had seen beat the cowering mass of flesh with a whip, while she cried out, begging for mercy.

Knowing it wasn't his place to step in between a dominant and his property, Damon could not stand by while the girl was beaten to a bloody pulp for an infraction that every slave is bound to make. Training is vital, and from what Damon had seen, nothing was implemented properly in the scenario. Growling low in his throat, he pauses to steady his now rapidly beating heart. What if *he,* had actually found her? What if *he* had made good on the threat the day at the court hearing? What if.. her abusive dominate HAD found her, even with all the precautions Damon had secured?

Moving from the office, across the room, Damon veers to the left and bursts into the master bath. Again, the shower and tub appear to have been freshly cleaned, with fresh towels put out in anticipation of a bath later. The scented soaking salts and lily molded bath soaps lying in wait in the dragon-shaped container on the side of the tub, awaiting their use. Waiting for Jewel.

Shaking his head clear of the thought, he moves back through the bedroom, glancing again at the way the room was left as if nothing had been out of sorts, as though it was just another day in the life of his Jewel. Moving down the hallway, Damon steps lightly as he swiftly descends the wooden stairs to the lower level of the house. Stepping onto the tiled foyer, he catches the sound of a muffled cry, turning his head slightly to the left, he eases himself toward the sold wooden cabinetry under the staircase.

Standing before the four-paned panel, he hears the sound of a slap against flesh. The realization dawns on his worried features, changing them from stress to annoyance as he presses the secret latch hidden under the lip of the paneling to open a hidden door. Catching the sound of a muffled moan, he moves quickly toward *the Dungeon,* His room, where only he, himself takes her when he wishes to use, abuse, and pleasure his pet, his property for his amusement and gratification. placing his palm flat against the wooden door, Damon lays an ear against the ornately engraved surface trying to catch any signs of who might be trespassing in what HE had made as a safe and comfortable place for Leigha.

Hearing the sound of a whip crack, followed by a muffled moan as the lash makes contact against flesh, causes Damon's caution to be thrown wayside. Slamming the door open, he moves swiftly into the dimly lit interior hall, the door to Narnia as Leigha lovingly refers to the short walk into the dungeon's main area. Stealthily moving the few steps with practiced silence, Damon hears the sound of a leather flogger connecting with naked flesh and the gagged silenced, high-pitched squeal of a woman. Throwing caution aside, he bursts into the room, stopping inches from the only means of safe escape.

Staring in disbelief at the two women before him, Damon's jaw drops open as his eyes make burning contact with the dark hazel orbs of his girl, the flogger held securely in her right hand, and the fingers of her left buried possessively in the dark triangle of a bound girl's cunt, whose flesh bears the unmistakable crisscrossing lines of flanges across her milky white skin.

Allowing his eyes to travel the girl's body, Damon's jaw tightens as his teeth grind with images flashing in his memory of nights spent with this girl now holding the flogger, as HE made those same identifiable marks on HER body. Letting his eyes come to rest on the bound girls' face, he wonders what it would be like to kiss those soft pink lips, now wrapped around one of his black silk gags, and have him place the unmistakable look of subspace on her lovely features.

Slowly forming a snarl with his lips curling away from white even teeth, Damon's dark blue eyes narrow dangerously, while he watches as Leigha slowly slides her manicured fingers from the girls' cunt, being sure to torment the already abused and sensitive flesh.

With her eyes glinting, a light begins to shine in Leigha's dark hazel eyes, her chin rising at a defiant angle as her eyes glow with an unspoken challenge.

'Oh yes, her training was obviously coming along just fine,' "What the hell?"

The whispered curse slips past Damon's sneering lips. Taking a deep breath, Leigha raises her chin proudly as she grasps the handle of the flogger with apparent practice.

"Master, I didn't expect you home so soon. I thought you were in Colorado on business."

The slight nervous surprise in Leigha's voice gives Damon little solace in what he's just stumbled upon.

"I was. Apparently, not in Colorado long enough. Slut."

Forcing the words past sneering lips, Damon stalks in a primal manner the few steps between himself and Leigha, quickly snatching a handful of her long hair in his fist, he twists the auburn tresses around his hand and forces her to her knees in front of him on the polished hard stone floor for her bound toy to see. Bending over slightly, he snatches the leather handle of the flogger, *HIS* flogger from Leigha's grasp.

Keeping his fingers firmly tangled in Leigha's long red-brown hair, Damon watches as the girl slowly focuses on the scene before her dazed vision. Looking into her shockingly blue eyes, his loins tighten with anticipation. Taking advantage of his dominance over Leigha, Damon caresses the young woman with his desire darkening eyes.

She's petite, and small, but rounded well in all the appropriate places. Barbie doll figures are not desirable to meet his needs. Allowing his eyes to wander from her bound bare feet, up her calves, he notices a beautifully designed tattoo of a black-winged unicorn on her outer left calf.

Raising his eyes higher, Damon admires the rounded hips above nicely muscled thighs, lingering on the dark patch of fur between her nicely opened legs, he admires the well-trimmed area, before raising his eyes to the softly rounded stomach, not too flat, just full enough to be pleasing.

Lifting his gaze past her ribcage, he is greeted by a stunning set of breasts. Well-rounded and perfectly designed for handling. Perky dark nipples, raised to taut attention from the cool temperature of the dungeon and the abuse Leigha has undoubtedly administered to the flesh.

Feeling his muscles twitch beneath the jean material of his pants, Damon lingers on her breasts, almost as beautiful as Leigha's, but to him, Leigha's body is perfection. Tearing his eyes away from the milky white flesh, he slowly roams up her neck, and over her jawline. Part of her face hidden beneath the silk gag, he searches the contours of her cheekbones, noting how lovely her face appears slightly flushed with use and desire.

Finally lifting his eyes to look into hers, the shade of blue, nearly knocks the breath from him. The raven wing black hair framing her form glistens a blue in the flickering Candle light from the sconces on the stone walls.

Noting that even with the long strands of black hair pulled back into a neat pony tail behind her head, the ends swing provocatively against her lower back. If the hair wasn't bound, he's sure it would fall past her full plump rear.

'This will definitely prove very interesting.'

The thought makes his eyes darken as he wonders how long his little slut has been actually training this toy while he's been absent on business trips. Glancing down at the woman kneeling at his feet in silent supplication, Damon smiles, as evil thoughts race through his mind. The thought of forcing his dear little submissive to watch as he uses his skill on her 'experiment' suddenly seems like a wonderfully, tantalizing idea.

Pulling Leigha's head forcefully back with her hair, Damon leans down into her face, lips nearly touching the corner of her softly pouting, pink mouth.

"She has a name, love?"

His question is met by a soft whimper, and with trembling lips, Leigha nods her head. Glancing in the direction of the still bound girl, Damon watches the bound girl twisting her wrists in the bonds uncomfortably, as her eyes dart from Leigha, then back to him. Looking for a sign of things to come, moving her wrists uncomfortably in the cuffs, he watches as she strains against the chains holding her arms above her head. Noting that her feet are firmly planted on the floor and bound to the rings at the ankles, he nods his head in complete admiration of his girl.

"You have learned well Jewel."

"Thank you, sir."

The whisper brings his attention back to the girl still clutched in his fingers. Narrowing his eyes, Damon releases Leigha's hair abruptly and watches as he falls into a crouch at his feet.

"Release the bitch, we..."

Looking from Leigha to the other, Damon indicates with a slight jerk of his head, that she is also included in the "we" part of the conversation.

"We have much to talk about."

Rising as quickly as possible from the hard floor, Leigha releases the now frightened girl. Whispering calming words to her, Leigha attempts to reassure the girl that Damon is not going to punish or harm her in any manner. If anything, it would be she, Leigha, receiving the brutal reprimand, and since coming to be with Master Drake, he has never once raised his hand against her flesh in anger.

Shutting the door and locking it, Damon turns on the two girls. Snapping his fingers, Leigha quickly takes her place at his feet.

"I am Damon, also referred to as Master Drake. I am unaware as to how much my slut has told you of me, but apparently, she has told you more than she has told me at this point. That we will sort out later. Your name please."

Looking from Damon to Leigha, the girl wrings her hands nervously and then swallows the sudden lump that has formed in her throat. Swallowing again, trying to rid herself of the oppressive object she opens her mouth, but no sound is forthcoming. Licking her lips, she keeps her head lowered as she senses Damon's eyes watching her every move.

"This girl is known as Raven, sir."

Raising a dark eyebrow, Damon is caught surprised to hear the use of the term, 'sir', As she then attempts to swallow the sudden lump as it is taught for lifestyle practices, to refer to herself in the third party. Obviously, something has been going on for some time. Looking at

Leigha, he watches as she lowers her head in shame. Or is it to hide that infuriating smirk she gets when she's proud of herself, or enjoying a cat and mouse game at his expense?

"My pleasure Raven."

Nodding her head slowly, Raven stands silently, with her head lowered and arms crossed over her naked mid-section. Knowing she has to be feeling more than a little awkward, Damon purses his lips attempting to quell the smile playing at the corners of his mouth.

"Seems my slut has been working with you for quite some time, you may sit."

"Thank you, master Drake."

Moving quietly with slight stiffness, she positions herself near enough to Leigha, but seemingly far enough away to feel safe from Damon's reach. Noting her choice of seating, Damon chuckles softly. Sighing, Damon, now taking on the full persona of Master Drake, paces the enclosed space of his dungeon, wondering what he is to do with his girl and newly acquired and deliciously looking morsel that has been offered into his lap.

Beginning to pace the room like a caged cat, Damon hears a slight noise from behind him, turning on his heel, he finds Leigha and Raven on their feet. Folding his arms across his muscular chest, Damon plants his feet firmly apart in his well-known dominant fashion. Watching the girls' boldly approach him, Damon looks from one to the other as he begins to wonder what is going through their devious minds.

Smiling wickedly up into his handsome face, each girl reaches out with both hands for his wrists, taking them both into velvety soft hands, narrowing eyes upon the girls, he shakes his head at them. With determination Leigha again takes his wrist in her hands.

"Allow us to prepare a bath master, we only wish to serve."

Narrowing dark eyes onto the pair, Damon quietly allows them to lead him into the dimly lit bathroom he had built recently into the dungeon. The scent of melting candles and flickering of burning flame draw his attention to the small room, looking from Leigha to Raven, Damon opens his mouth as though to speak. Quickly placing her hand over his mouth, Leigha stills the very thought of speech. Deciding to play this game a little longer, Damon's curiosity has been peeked. Shaking her head in denial, Leigha leads Damon into the close confines of the bathing room. Entering the room Raven quickly shuts the door and slides the bolt into place.

Glancing back, Damon stares dumbly at the new bolt, He wasn't the one who installed the blasted lock, but he sure as hell would be the one to remove it, … possibly.

Closing and locking the door, Leigha and Raven slowly converge on Damon and start removing his shirt, first unbuttoning the small dress buttons lining the front of his dark blue dress shirt. Their soft hands brush against his chest and arms as they slide the material from his body. Standing, Damon side-eyes Leigha, as she places her hands on her hips, a devious smile curling her pretty lips.

"Remove your pants, Drake, I want to see your naked flesh before me."

Looking down into Leigha's face, Damon laughs. The sound reverberating against the stone walls of the small room.

"Who the hell do you think you are cunt? I'm lord and master here."
"Not tonight you aren't Drake."

The soft command draws Damon's eyes to meet the haughty gaze of his slave. Holding her head at a defiant angle, she watches the menacing change wash over Damon. Noticing the tightening of his jaw, the narrowing of his eyes, and the color of the blue of the iris, change from an amusing light blue to a deep almost black color in appearance. Leigha wonders if perhaps this little stunt was not very well thought out.

As he attempts to reach out with his long arm and strong fingers to snatch her slender upper arm, he hears a sharp hiss and the instant feel of the sting of a whip Quickly strike from behind. Having the whips cord wrapped snuggly around his neck instantly cuts his ability to breathe in half. Cursing under his breath, Damon's angry gaze of blackened pupils' rests on Leigha. The lash of *his* whip, wrapped around *HIS* neck seems impossible.

'How the hell had he not been aware of this sluts' actions?'

Backing down slightly, Damon balls his hands into fists, takes a steadying breath, and slowly unfastens the button of his jeans and releases the zipper. Allowing the heavy jean material to fall from his hips, Leigha watches the material pool in a heap at his feet. Smiling at the sight of his pure nakedness before her, Leigha reaches out to stroke Damon's thigh with her well-manicured fingertips, causing the hair on his legs to rise on end with the goose-pimpled flesh.

Watching the muscles of his face relax, Leigha smiles as Damon's eyes slowly flutter closed and a moan passes his lips.

"Did I say you could speak?"

A fast crack against his thigh snaps Damon's eyes open. Staring in disbelief at Leigha, he snarls dangerously but quickly conceals the glare of doom in his storm-darkened eyes, and assuming the part of submissive, he clamps his teeth shut and averts his gaze to the floor. Biting his tongue against the snide unspoken comment, Damon waits.

"That's better. To your knees boy."

Kicking his feet out of the pool of material, Damon raises his eyes the color of pitch black to his kajira, his slave. Watching Damon slowly sink down onto his knees on the cool stone floor, Leigha watches every muscle tense in his beautiful frame, the strong muscles in his upper chest flex with each fist he forms at his sides.

"Apologize to your domme, boy."

The softly spoken command coming from behind him surprises Damon, the mouse he had seen in the dungeon is no mouse at all. Getting no response from this handsome man kneeling on the floor,

Raven tugs slightly on the lash still wrapped around Damon's throat. Bringing his head up, he stares defiantly at Leigha.

'Of all the arrogant, pigheaded, hair-brained women!'

Attempting to rise, his only thought is to wrap his hands around Leigha's neck and bring the little bitch to her knees. The sudden pull against the whips lashes still wrapped around his throat stop Damon from his attempted desire of getting to his feet, cursing under his breath he raises brutally defiant eyes to Leigha, seeing the love shining in her darkened green eyes, Damon feels as though someone has punched him in the gut. Knocking the wind from the violent tirade he was planning to unleash on this woman. Softening his own deathly stare, Damon lowers his eyes to the floor as he's trained his slave to do in submission. Cupping Damon's face gently with her hand, Leigha feels his lips caress her palm in a silent apology. Using his tongue to trace small circles in the center of her palm, she finds herself completely intoxicated by the warm moistness of the tip of his tongue against her skin. Pulling her hand slowly away from Damon's mouth, she traces her manicured fingertip along his roughened jawline to the delicate shell of his ear.

Softly tracing the contours of the shell-shaped ear, Leigha slips her fingers into the thick dark mass of Damon's hair. Leaning over slightly she gently kisses the top of his bowed head. Sharing a secret glance with Raven over the top of Damon's head, Leigha moves slowly away from him and smiles gently into his face. Her heart nearly skipped several beats with the love and desire she has for her master. Even knowing at some point, she will pay for this wicked game.. and pay dearly.

Swallowing the lump in her throat, Leigha turns her attention to Raven. "Rise and bathe Damon. Raven, assist him, girl. I want him cleansed."

Watching Raven carefully unwrap the whips' leather lash still snaked around Damon's throat, Leigha indicates with a nod of her head for the girl to kneel beside the tub. Taking her place in the wingback chair placed in the corner of the room, Leigha silently enjoys the relaxing sound of the water sloshing and running in the tub as Raven begins to prepare for Damon's bath.

Glancing at the tub, Raven indicates to Damon with a wave of her hand, it is time for him to enter the tub Smiling a hungry sneer, Leigha watches Damn carefully step into the steamy bath water and closes her eyes to the relaxing sound of the water in the tub. Leigha watches silently as Raven begins bathing his sculptured form, the water glistening in the candle light as it runs down his body.

Watching in complete silence, Leigha begins to rub her braless nipples through the sheer blouse hanging loosely on her thin frame, knowingly antagonizing Damon as she is fully aware of the pleasure this action brings him to watch.

Purposely sliding her hand down her flat stomach, Leigha slides her delicate fingers over her wet crotch, dipping a finger between her pussy lips the light material of her skirt outlines the shape of her cunt and emphasizes the shadow of fur covering her genital area. Leigha's eyes narrow as she watches Damon's mouth gap slightly, then suddenly snap shut to swallow the saliva forming in his mouth.

As Raven continues to soap his body, Leigha watches as her hands move expertly over Damons' wet skin with the cloth, leaving a soap trail along his thighs and down exquisitely muscled legs.

"See to it you wash him completely slut. Leave nothing untouched."

Hearing the quick intake of breath, Leigha lazily travels her dark eyes up Damon's body to his face.

"Nothing untouched, I want you clean."

The dangerous darkening expression stops Leigha for an instant, licking her lips nervously, she pulls her bottom lip in between her teeth and gnaws it gently, wondering if perhaps she has pushed too far. Never has her master given such quarter before, perhaps this should end?

Dropping her eyes from his expression, her stubborn will kicks in, and raising her face to meet his glowering expression, Leigha knows there is no turning back, it has begun. She's been planning this for months, sneaking about training his new toy. Yes, this continues, regardless of the punishment.

Hearing the words uttered from Leigha's lips, Damon's expression grows dangerous, and thinking silently...

'Where has he heard those very same words? AH yes, HE spoke them to these very same girl years before, when he brings her to her first training session. Yes, she shall pay dearly.'

Waiting for an explosive denial from Damon's lips, Leigha nods her head as he drops his in submission to the command.

"Very wise Drake, you are learning my love."

Daring to raise his head slightly, Damon looks directly to Leigha, with dangerously narrowed eyes, a low rumble of a chuckle barely escapes his throat, as the corners of his mouth lift in a slight joker's grin.

"You have no clue as to what monster you have just unleashed my beautifully daring slut."

Letting the cloth fall from her instantly limp fingers, she silently obeys Leigha's soft order. Lessening the grip on her wrist, Leigha seems pleased to see how well her training is beginning to take effect.

"Yes Milady, as you wish,"

Releasing her wrist, Leigha places a finger under her chin and gently pulls Raven to meet gently lips. Setting her lips against Raven's, Leigha engages her in a soft, sensuous kiss. Hearing Damon moan from above Leigha deepens the kiss, teasing Raven's bottom lip until the girl opens her lips, allowing Leigha to take full possession of her mouth.

Shoving her tongue into Raven's mouth, Leigha hears an audible gasp from above them, and breaks the kiss from Raven's lips. Glancing up at Damon with a "what" type expression, Leigha nods her head with a chin lift to indicate Raven is to continue with Damons' scrub down.

Moving back to her seat, Leigha, sits with legs slightly spread, the open gap of the blouse hiding nothing from view. Watching her with a stormy expression, Damon swallows the saliva filling his mouth. Raising an eyebrow and a slight mouth quirk, Leigha motions with a finger for Damon to sit in the warm tub.

"I figure you would prefer to sit, rather than stand in the cool room."

Not daring to speak, Damon sits to allow Raven to continue bathing him. Rising from her chair, Leigha again comes to the side of the tub, and sliding her hand up Damon's wet, soapy thigh, she intentionally bumps the tightened sack resting below Damon's rigid cock. Taking the orb into her palm, she squeezes his knot sack gently, pulling against the tightened flesh as a shiver race through his body.

Sliding her hand over the sack, and onto his standing member, Leigha wraps her long fingers around the tight muscle. Stroking from base to head, she rolls her palm over the soft velvety ball of the head of Damon's cock, causing it to jump at her gentle touch.

Rolling her fingers over the tip, Leigha dips the tip of one of her fingers into the slit at the top of Damon's member. Sliding her finger off the head of his dick, she finds a slimy string of pre-cum attached to her fingertip. The heat between her legs, causes a moan to escape her throat, leaning towards Raven, Leigha meets the girl's willing mouth, sliding her tongue against Raven's lips, Leigha smiles slightly as Raven complies with the gentle request and snakes her tongue into the girls' willing mouth, possessing it, claiming her.

Stroking Damon's cock to the base, Leigha releases his member and revels in the control she has at this moment in time. Slipping the fingers of her free hand into the dark strands of Raven's ponytail, Leigha grips the base of the ponytail into her fist, using the base of the tail to control Raven's shimmering dark locks, she pulls the girl's head back gently to break the kiss between them. Raven's eyes remain as Leigha trails warm, moist kisses down her jaw. The soft sound of a tortured moan brings a wicked grin to Leigha's lips as she gently releases Raven from the spell woven around the girls' dazed senses.

Looking over to Damon, Leigha traces the contours of his face with dark green eyes. Following the curve of Damon's jaw, she traces a path with her eyes down his throat and past his collarbone to lazily caress his muscular chest and abdomen in the soapy water, until coming to rest on the now rigid cock standing boldly before him.

Reaching out once again to Damon, Leigha wraps her hand around his throbbing cock and strokes it leisurely with deliberate slow strokes, imitating the times when he would do such torment to her during a lengthy session. Taking his time with her body, driving her into complete madness before allowing her the release she so desperately begged for.

Damons' moan tells Leigha that any control he thought he had, is slipping from his grasp. Using her palm to caress the head of his cock, she then rubs her fingernails over the head of his cock, then using her nails, she then drags her nails over the head of Damon's flesh, feeling the warmth of his cum seeping from the slit in the velvety soft head. Pulling away from him, Leigha bites her bottom lip, as she looks up into the black eyes of her master, watching her intently.

Nodding to Raven, Leigha wipes the soap and water from her hand and returns to lounging in the chair next to the tub she was seated in earlier. Watching as Damon continues to grit his teeth and clench his hands into tight fists, Leigha grins crookedly as her master attempts to remain in control of his own body.

"Drake, stand."

The spoken order, brings dark, dangerous eyes to rest on Leigha, gripping the sides of the tub, Damon rises fluidly from the tub of water, and the sound of water sloshing over the sides of the claw-legged porcelain tub causes Raven to squeal in surprise.

Watching as Damon again balls his hands into fists, Leigha grins crookedly as her master struggles to remain standing as Raven's soft hands lather his inner thighs and slowly work toward his cock. Slipping her fingers between Damon's ass cheeks, Shauna glances quickly at Leigha, who in turn nods to continue the task. Watching every muscle in Damon's body tense, Leigha clicks her tongue gently, A soft warning, to allow the girl to do her job as ordered.

Making a soft clicking sound with her tongue, Leigha shakes her head and uses a finely manicured finger to point toward the floor. Dropping his eyes, Damon slowly bends forward, allowing Raven's fingers to slip over the tightly puckered hole of his anus as Leigha meets cleanses his body. Rubbing her hands between his legs from behind, her palms rub lightly against the tightened ball sack just under his cock, sending chills over his entire body. A soft chuckle from Leigha nearly brought Damon to his knees, a harsh hiss and ragged breathing his only reply to the new sensations coursing through his lean muscular frame.

Daring to glance in Leigha's direction, Damon watches as she raises her head slightly, cocking an eyebrow at his obvious defiance. The single look alone says more than a hundred words could speak. Watching Damon drop his head in submission, Leigha smiles slightly as she settles back to watch Raven continue her administration to Damons' body.

Standing with jaw-clenched and trembling legs, Damon gasps as Raven's hand slowly caresses his throbbing cock. Stroking the member in a rotating motion around the velvety head of his dick, Raven glances up to watch his reaction. Moaning an animalistic sound before his trembling body causes him to crumble to his knees in the chilled water of the tub.

Rising quickly from her seat, Leigha snatches a towel from the nearby hanger and hands it to Raven, Knowing Damon is surely tested past his limits and not knowing when the last time was he actually submitted to another, Leigha doesn't wish to waste time or lose him before the session has even begun.

"Get out Drake my sweet, I am not finished with you as of yet."

Shaking his head slowly, Damon looks to Leigha, a change has come over him, a softening of sorts. His breathing is rapid and his body trembles as Raven dumps warm water over his naked body to remove any soap residue.

"Dommina... my Mistress...this slave can't refrain.. I can't take more." His raspy, tortured plea brings Leigha to his side at the tub. "Yes you can Drake, you can do this, my love."

Shakily stepping from the tub, Damon stands next to Raven as she offers the towel for him to wrap around his tightly sculptured waist. Still trembling, Damon wraps the towel snuggly around his slim hips, Turning to look at Leigha, he notices the black strip of cloth grasped in her hand. Slowly shaking his head, a mutinous threat clouds his dark eyes as Leigha nods her head. Feeling the firm, but gentle grip of Raven's hand on his wrist, Damon finds his wrists being bound with one of the woven hemp ropes from his extensive collection in the dungeon. The course rawness of the hemp, warns Damon to forget any struggles, any noticeable burns or marks caused by such material, would be hard to explain to his employers.

"Turn around love, 'tis time for my pleasure."

As Damon turns, Leigha can only imagine the glare cast in Ravens' direction as her face breaks into a wide smile and she lifts her hands up, wrists together as if she too, were bound by some invisible binding. Stepping onto the stool, Leigha places the black, silk blindfold over Damon's eyes. As his vision becomes completely impaired, a low growl escapes his throat. Sudden memories flood his mind's eye, the thrill of being bound and helpless adds to his already barely manageable desire. Trying to stamp the flood of memories, Damon suddenly envisions the face of his only mistress, the one that opened his eyes to the world of his becoming a dominant, a master, a Dominus in the making.

Taking hold of the towel wrapped around Damon's body, Leigha snaps the terry cotton cloth from his tapered waist, exposing his beautifully formed body. Unlocking the bathroom door, she opens it, allowing a rush of cold air to kiss Damon's still-damp body as he's led slowly and carefully back into the outer dungeon.

Giving softly spoken direction, Damon is led through the cool dungeon to the far corner of the room where the 'Masters' bed awaits in the dim area against the stone wall of the chamber. Resting her warm hands on Damon's hips, Leigha helps keep Damon balanced as he's guided toward the corner. Being told to kneel, he slowly goes to his knees as he feels the side of the mattress make contact with his legs. Allowing his weight to sink fully onto the mattress, he suddenly feels a solid push against his shoulders as Raven or Leigha force him onto the bed, rolling to his side onto the soft, silky comforter, Damon adjusts his positioning onto his back. Resting his bound wrists against his midsection, his body flexes with the motion of the mattress as it shifts with his weight. Uncertain as to what's going on around him, he wonders if this is how Leigha felt when first placed in this very same position when at his hands for the first time.

Taking a breath, he shifts his weight squarely onto his back, feeling soft hands beginning to roam across his legs, Damon tenses slightly. The feeling of helplessness in his position sends a thrill of excitement through his body, he'd felt this once when he was under the tutelage of the dominatrix, Lady J, who taught him to become the master he is now.

Hearing the sound of the chain tethers being lifted from the posts of the massive four poster wooden bed, Damon shakes his head back and forth against the pillow his head is resting on.

"Leigha....."

The softly spoken sound of her name brings Leigha's attention to the man lying on the large bed, a shiver races down her spine as she has never heard her name spoken in such a menacing growl before. Glancing at Raven, she silently nods her head for the girl to continue binding Damon's ankles in the wool-lined leather ankle cuffs, that he so much enjoys using on her while dolling out his pleasure.

Moving as quietly as possible to Damon's head, Leigha lays her soft cheek against his, rubbing her soft skin against his neatly trimmed beard.

"Yes, master?"

Her voice whispered so softly in his ear causes Damon's breath to catch in his throat, the feel of her warm breath against his ear makes his cock twitch with a sudden desire to be touched. The flirtatious lilt in her voice causes his heart to rap against his rib cage, never had she given him the slightest notion, the slightest hint towards the fact she was learning to dominate while learning to submit.

The feel of the ankle cuff being tightened against his flesh draws Damon from his musings.

"Don't continue this journey slut. The outcome may not be what you envision my love."

The soft chuckle in his ear, makes Damon groan. With Raven finishing the binding of Damon's ankles, Leigha slides her hands across the soft fur covering Damon's chest, his muscles rippling under her fingertips with her light, delicate touch. Kissing the space just in front of his ear, she trails the tip of her tongue over the outline of his ear. Knowing how much he finds the action disorienting, she smiles slightly when his head tips towards his left shoulder to attempt to avoid the action.

Smiling against his ear, Leigha kisses a slow moist trail down Damon's jawline to the corner of his mouth. Feeling his breath fan her face, she realizes his breathing is more rapid than she's ever noticed before, he's not in control, and he's unable to obtain the place where his dominant side stays.

Kissing the corner of Damon's mouth, Damon is slow to respond to her gentle touch. Slipping her tongue across Damon's lips until he relinquishes his stubborn resolve and opens his mouth to her insistent persuasion. Dipping the tip of her tongue between his lips, she licks the inner side of his lips in a teasing motion.

Groaning softly, he raises his head to follow her retreating mouth. Resting her lips against his, Leigha takes his mouth in a possessive kiss, her lips melting into the flesh of his full soft kiss, while her tongue snakes into his mouth to taste the essence of his desire.

Teasing his tongue with hers, Leigha softly moans as Damon lifts his bound hands to slip the back of his hand along her rib cage. His need to touch, evident in the desire to make contact with her body. Breaking the kiss, Leigha lingers slightly over his lips as Damon's breath fans her face, in uncontrolled pants.

Kissing his lips once more, she slides her cool fingers tips down his neck, to his left nipple. Rolling the upraised hardened peck between her thumb and forefinger, Leigha hears the soft intake of breath as Damon flexes his pectoral muscle attempting to evade the tender torment of her fingers gently pinching the hardened tip.

Sliding her fingertips down the center of Damon's chest, she slips across his sternum. Down the middle of his torso, following the path of soft fur to his belly button. Leigha glides her fingers around the rim of the alcove, before running her soft fingers further down the furry path of his stomach. Coming into contact with the coarse pubic hair framing his genital area, she splays her fingers wide open to allow the tightly curled hair to slip through them with ease.

Rubbing the palm of her hand against his flattened pubic hair, her fingers rake against the hardened flesh of his cock. Rocking his hips slightly to give Leigha better access to his throbbing member, Wrapping her fingers around the thick, vein-lined flesh, Leigha strokes Damon's rod from base to head and then back down his shaft. Raising his hips into her hand, Damon growls deep in his throat.

Removing her hand from his rod, Leigha cups the tightened sack beneath his cock and rolls the fleshy ball in her palm. Jerking his legs in frustration, Damon attempts to buck the slender form off his body by raising his shoulders in an attempt to roll partially to his side.

The soft giggle above him, only manages to anger Damon as he again vainly attempts to roll the individual off his chest. In one swift motion, the warmth of the body disappears from his chest, only to end up straddling his face. The heated scent of sex and desire fills Damon's nostrils as the moist, delicate flesh of a woman's sex covers his mouth.

Shocked momentarily, Damon inhales deeply and is assaulted by the sweet scent of strawberries and sex. The warm feel of soft thighs against cheeks, nearly causes his undoing. Opening his lips against the softly rocking hips, Damon finds her settling herself deeper against his mouth. The open invitation too much to refuse, he snakes his tongue out against the moist layers of the intoxicating pussy placed in his mouth.

The taste of cunt, mingled with a tinge of strawberry has Damon completely lost over his senses. Using his tongue to whip around the tight bud of the clitoris, he sucks the tender flesh between his teeth, nibbling gently. Lapping his tongue between the folds of skin, he sucks the swollen pussy lips of the person sitting on his face between his own lips.

Knowing the feel and taste of Leigha, Damon quickly assumes this must be Raven. Nibbling on the clit once again, her hips rock forward in a silent plea for his tongue to dip into the recess of her cunt. Her flavor was a bit tangier than of his Leigha, but still ever so inviting.

Attempting to raise his hands up, Damon considers touching the lower back and hip region of this girl so brazenly sitting atop his face, when the crisp click of a clasp against the bindings stop his hand's ascent. The cool chain falls heavily against his stomach and groin region.

Smiling slightly against Raven's flesh, he sucks her wet, tender, over sensitized flesh into his mouth. His teeth pinch down on the sensitive flesh. Squealing slightly, Raven gasps and grabs a hand full of his thick hair, pushing against his forehead, she shoves his head deeper into the soft pillow, forcing Damon to release her skin abruptly.

"Bastard!..."

The soft admonishment brings a slight grin to Damon's lips. Climbing off his chest, Raven moves quietly off the bed as Leigha takes Damon's cock in her warm, moist mouth. Inhaling with the pleasure of his girls' mouth on his cock, Damon rocks his hips upward to invite her to take the entire rod into her mouth. Feeling the back of her throat touch the head of his dick, Damon rolls his hips to the head of his cock slips past her gag reflex, and into her throat, swallowing his cock, Leigha's lips touch the base of Damon's pubic area. The hair tickles her nose and lips as she swallows his rod, rising off his throbbing member, she caresses the tightened, bulging cock with her teeth, from base to head.

Humming as she slides off Damon's cock, Leigha licks the head of his cock as if it were a lollipop. Sliding her tongue over the velvet tip, she then dips the tip of her tongue into the slit of his cock to taste the slimy pre-cum seeping from Damon's cock head. Rising from the bed, Leigha instructs Raven to mount Damon's face once again as she, herself mounts Damon's cock.

Positioning herself over Damon's mouth, Raven settles herself against his eager lips. Feeling them press against her pussy, she moans softly and rocks forward slightly so Damon can have complete access to her womanhood. Slipping her fingers through his thick hair, she lets her head fall back on her shoulders so her long black tress's hang low against her back, falling past her hips to pool at the ends in the center of Damon's chest.

Moaning into her pussy, Damon sucks the sensitive flesh between his teeth to gently gnaw on swollen lips. The quick intake of air signals her enjoyment at the action, using his tongue, he swirls around the tightened bud and her clitoris. Pulling against the chain holding his hands at bay, Damon growls lowly with the desire to touch snow-white flesh.

Rocking her hips slightly, Raven grinds her pussy deeper against Damon's mouth, dipping his tongue into the recess of her cunt he feels her body shudder with the unexpected climax.

Hearing her gasp in surprise, he quickly understands that she is completely new to the "lifestyle" and all it has to offer. Tasting her juice on his tongue, Damon suckles against the flesh until Raven quickly rises from his mouth.

"Mistress?"

The soft begging lilt to her voice, makes Damon wonder what these two are up to. Waiting silently, he swallows the saliva forming in his mouth, the taste of Ravens' climax still fresh on his tongue.

"You belong to me, Shauna, my love,, my Raven. Your body is mine to command, to control as I so desire."

A shudder races through Damon's body as Leigha slips her wet cunt over the head of his cock. Her flesh resting against his as she sits on top of his groin, rocking slightly so the head of his cock penetrates her cunt and rubs against the deep area of inner flesh containing her "g" spot.. Sighing from the pleasure of being on Damon's cock, Leigha rocks her hips in practiced motion to bring herself to a powerful, breathtaking climax.

Her moans fill Damon's ears as his cock fills her cunt. Feeling Raven rise from his chest, Damon can do nothing but wait at the mercy of this woman, the woman he's allowed to take control of his body, his mind.

Leaning forward onto Damon's chest, Leigha captures Damon's mouth in a savage, desire driven kiss. Her tongue delving deeply into his mouth as she traces the contours of his tongue with hers, the taste of Raven still on his tongue, Leigha wages war on Damon's senses.

Rising slowly from his lap, Leigha slowly dismounts from the pleasure of Damon's cock. Feeling soft fingers encircle his solid member, a moan slips past his lips. Nipping Damon's bottom lip, Leigha strokes the side of his face. Tracing her fingers through his hair and pulling his face closer to her, Damon can smell the fragrance of Leigha's body lotion and the musky scent of her arousal. Slipping her fingers across Damon's lips, Leigha slides a finger between his lips, as Damon takes the offered digit, he takes a deep breath and tastes the familiar flavor of his slut. Her sweet, musky taste. One he's very acquainted with, she's masturbated, or at least been dipping her finger into her cunt so she could offer her flavor to his mouth.

Feeling his member throb, Damon sucks on the finger offered to him. Removing her finger from between his lips, Leigha touches his lips to her skin, the soft feel of her neck arouses Damon to the point of distraction. Not in years has he allowed his defenses to go down. Not since leaving mistress J, after his domination of her. The last night they spent together was one he would never forget, the domination of her, her domination of him, the hours spent making love, memorizing every contour of each other's bodies. The night she released him.

Having his cock throbbing in the soft silky hands of Raven, her strokes become bolder as they follow the length of his flesh, rubbing the head and stroking the rod from the head to the base of the shaft. Feeling the bed shift slightly under the change of weight of the two women, Damon groans with the release of Ravens' hand from his cock and the sudden loss of Leigha's body next to his.

Suddenly realizing that maybe this is how Leigha may have felt during her training, what she's doing to him is reminiscent of how she was treated while in preparatory training to become his. Feeling a twinge of regret, Leigha's touch brings him back to the moment as her fingers stroke his calves and drift up his thighs to flutter across his rigid cock.

Lingering shortly, Leigha strokes his dick with soft hands, feeling his hardened cock throb at her touch, she crawls over Damon, straddling his hips with her body. A growl slips past Damon's lips as his control begins to waiver, and his hips appear to have a mind of their own as they rock against Leigha's body, begging for more.

Chuckling softly as she continues to crawl up his body until she's sitting on his chest, the heat of her crotch seeming to sear his chest.

Leaning over him, Leigha's wispy blouse brushes against Damon's face, and the soft fragrance of her body lotion assails his senses.

Frustration fills him as he silently screams to have the blindfold removed, and the desire to beg begins to fill his mind. Sitting comfortably on Damon's chest, Leigha keeps most of her weight on bended knee.

"Now boy, what shall I do with you?"

Leaning down she gently kisses him on the mouth, lingering as her tongue slips into the warm recess of his mouth. Deepening the kiss, she sucks his tongue into her mouth, inciting a soft muffled moan. Breaking the kiss, Leigha rises from Damon's chest, letting a smile play across her lips as she bends down and kisses the head of his cock, tasting the saltiness of his cum on the velvety head.

Rocking his hips toward Leigha, she allows his cock to slip into her mouth, scraping her teeth down the length of the shaft and back to the tip, where she swirls her tongue around the seeping head.

Clamping her teeth against the throb of his cock, she grates her teeth down to the base, and back up to the head, Damon's moan fills the room as he jerks against the bonds holding him at bay.

Arching his back, Damn lifts his hips from the bed, forcing his cock deeper into Leigha's mouth. Suckling the head of his cock, Leigha dips the tip of her tongue into the tight slit of his cock.

Clenching his haw, Damon fights the desire to explode. Clenching his fists, he pulls against the bonds, making the chain rattle against itself. The sound of creaking wood, warns Leigha of just how close Damon is to losing all control.

"Leigha, please."

The sound of Damon's tortured request fuels Leigha sucking the head of his cock into her warm mouth, his taste envelopes her senses as she continues the gentle torment on his sensitive flesh. Swallowing the velvety flesh deep into her throat, she feels the throb of his cock inside her throat and swallows convulsively before pulling off the head of his cock.

Licking the saliva from the velvety tip, she caresses the head of his cock with her tongue. Caressing the head of his cock with her tongue, Leigha hears the beginning of soft begging, realizing he's forgotten his place, Damon has fallen into complete submission.

Caressing the head of his member with her tongue, she suckles the seeping cum off the head of his dick, and listens as softly whispered words fill the quiet room. The soft begging brings a chuckle to her throat.

"You forget your place boy, keep your begging silent."

Watching Damon's face tighten at her command, Leigha knows how hard this must be for Damon, he was not one to keep his tongue in check. But then again, why should he? He was after, the Dominate, her master.. Smiling to herself, Leigha nods her head at Raven, instructing her to come forward while Leigha sits back and watches.

Raven begins a slow leisurely stroke of Damon's cock, her hands working wonderfully against Damon's tightened flesh, as she slowly strokes his cock and fondles his scrotum her long black hair brushes against his leg, Leigha hears the quick intake of breath as Ravens' soft full mouth covers his throbbing member.

With Raven's hand stroking the hardened shaft in the opposite direction of her mouth, Leigha sits, watching as Raven pulls back down on Damon's cock. Her hand going down his shaft as her mouth strokes upward, toward the now purple head of his aching rod, moving slowly against his flesh, Raven teases the swollen head with her tongue. Flicking the course, moist texture of her tongue across the tip of his cock. Lapping eagerly at the opening slit, suckling the head, and taking it fully into her mouth.

Watching Raven from her place at Damon's side, Leigha sits quietly as Raven administers Damon's cock. Her own mouth watering from the sensuality of the scene, reaching out to pinch a taught nipple, Leigha twists it slightly before releasing the tortured flesh. Damon's gasp brings a slow smile to Leigha's lips and she rubs the insulted area of Ravens' nipple, only to lightly pinch the tightened nub again. Arching his body against the bonds holding him, a soft growl escapes Damon's lips as Leigha watches the torment taking its toll on his body.

Tossing his head side to side, the soft panting tells her how truly arouse, and tormented Damon really is. The sounds of the mattress creaking, blend with the sounds of his moans, and the soft murmurs from Ravens' mouth against his stiff rod. Sliding her hand up Damon's neck, Leigha encircles his neck with her slender fingers applying gentle pressure to still his movements and moaning. Her fingers tighten slightly against his skin and she can feel the throb of his heart under her fingertips, the very life source coursing through his veins.

Leaning down next to Damon's ear, Leigha's tongue traces the lobe, her lips barely touching the sensitive flesh. Suckling his ear into her mouth, Damon's moan fills the room. Nipping his ear lobe slightly, Leigha smiles against his ear as a surprised gasp escapes his throat. Jerking his head away from the torment, Damon freezes as the gentle grip on his throat suddenly tightens, restricting his breathing slightly.

Clicking her tongue in admonishment, Leigha pinches his nipple while increasing the pressure until his moan satisfies her need for discipline. Leigha watches Raven continue to suckle Damon's cock, her head bobbin up and down as suckling sounds fill the room with her mouth moving faster, sliding up and down faster as Leigha instructs her to stroke his shaft with her hand. Fondling his ball sack with long fingers, Leigha slides her hand down his side, ad over his hip onto his sack, replacing Ravens gentle touch with her firmer grip.

Damon's soft gasp brings yet another satisfied grin to Leigha's lips as she begins to knead the tightened flesh of his scrotum, touching Raven's shoulder, Leigha moves to Raven's side and quickly trades places with Raven, by placing her mouth on Damon's cock in place of Ravens'.

Swallowing his cock, she gently grates her teeth up the shaft to the head, nipping it cruelly, the sudden jerk and grunt from his body please

Leigha greatly. Still fondling his sack with her long fingers, she takes his cock deeply into her mouth, tasting the salty cum against her tongue.

Rocking his hips into Leigha's face, she takes the length of Damon's cock into her mouth. Releasing his sack, she keeps sucking his cock as she reaches over to gently fondle the nearby breast of Raven. Suckling the head of his cock, Leigha laps the slit in the center of the head of Damon's cock, releasing Raven's breast, Leigha instructs her to remove the blindfold from Damon's eyes, with a flip of her hand.

Doing as instructed, Raven gently removes the cloth covering his eyes. Giving his sight time to adjust, Leigha quietly lays her leg across his while leisurely stroking his cock. Slipping a pillow under his head, Damon finds himself able to view what is happening in the lower region of the bed.

Smiling wickedly, Leigha again sucks his cock harshly into her mouth, letting her teeth scrape the hard muscle of his dick and forcing a ragged moan from his lips. Releasing his cock from her mouth, she slowly strokes the throbbing rod. Moving against Raven, Leigha traces her fingers along the contour of the girl's shoulder, letting her fingers lightly graze Raven's delicate jaw line.

Slipping her fingers into the girl's hair at the base of her neck, Leigha tangles her fingers into the long tresses and pulls her slowly into her. Allowing her lips to lightly touch Ravens' cheek, she slowly kisses a trail to her mouth. Lingering against soft pink lips, Leigha kisses her gently, moving her tongue across the girl's slightly gaping mouth.

Tracing the outline of Ravens' mouth with her tongue, Leigha tastes the sweetness of her essence. Slipping her tongue into Raven's willing mouth, Leigha closes her lips against Raven's mouth, while savoring the gentleness and softness against her skin. Deepening the kiss, she feels the texture of her mouth against Leigha's tongue, sexually exciting her, the sound of her breathing becoming raspy, speaks volumes to Leigha, as she sucks Raven's tongue into her mouth, while still slowly stroking Damon's hot, throbbing cock.

Releasing Raven from the kiss, Leigha abruptly releases Damon's cock, Leigha breaks the kiss between her and Raven, to begin a leisurely path down her body with soft hands. Glancing toward Damon, Leigha is pleased to see that he is still seemingly entranced with the actions. Moving away from Raven, Leigha lifts the leather flogger from the bed, letting the cool leather of the floggers' flanges slide against his thigh and over his cock. Staring intently into Damon's face, Leigha dangles the flogger over his erection, watching his eyes widen slightly at the realization of her actions, Damon clenches his hands into tight fists as she watches him as a cat would watch a mouse.

A slow smile plays across her lips as she rubs the flanges against his thigh and over his throbbing cock, causing it to jump at the contact of soft leather against his vulnerable flesh. Slowly dragging the leather strips up his body, she can sense the thrill behind the dangerously darkened eyes.

Swinging the flogger suddenly, it makes sharp contact with his thigh, just below the hard erection. A gasp catches in Damon's throat from the slight sting of the leather against his flesh. Raising the leather again, Leigha brings it down against the other thigh, rendering the flesh to a soft pink. Rubbing her soft hand against the offended area, she watches Damon's eyes close slowly.

Her fingers barely touching the now, visibly throbbing erection of Damon's desire, the feel of blood pumping through his skin, she grips his cock, and while squeezing slightly, begins stroking his flesh from base to head. Leigha's palm rubs the velvety tip. Coming into contact with the slit at the center of the head, her palm becomes coated with the slick wetness of pre-cum, raising her hand away from Damon's cock, he helplessly watches as Leigha turns to Raven and commands the girl in gentle tones to lick his cum from Leigha's offered palm.

As her warm tongue comes into contact with Leigha's pal, Damon's low growl draws her attention. Cocking an eyebrow, Leigha's dark green eyes seem to bore into Damon's soul. Letting her head drop slightly to the side, she looks to Damon with little more than mild interest.

With Ravens' mouth still against her palm, Leigha drops the flogger onto the bed between Damon's open thighs, the leather instrument bouncing slightly against his throbbing erection.

Raising her free hand to Raven's chin, Leigha raises Raven's face to hers. Glancing at Damon once more to ensure he's watching, Leigha draws the entranced girl closer and slowly places her lips against white pliant flesh. Tasting the saltiness of Damon's cum still on her soft kiss swollen lips, Leigha deepens the kiss until her tongue fills Raven's mouth as she clings to Leigha, whimpering with desire.

Feeling the bed jerk, Leigha breaks the kiss and lifts the flogger from between Damon's thighs. Gripping the handle securely, Leigha brings the strips down against Damon's upper thigh once again. The sudden sting causes Damon to pull against the leather cuffs holding him securely with chains to the wooden head board of the large bed.

An animalistic moan escapes his throat as the flogger comes down against Damon's muscled flesh, soft pleas of sexual hunger linger in the room.

"Please Mistress, please release me."

The softly moaned plea sounds breathless in the quiet room, taking Damon's cock into her hand, Leigha commands Raven to come to her. Having Raven cover Damon's body with her warm flesh, Leigha guides Damon's cock into Ravens' vagina, taking advantage of the extremely moist area, Leigha slips a finger into Raven along with Damon's cock, and she can feel Ravens' moistness envelop his stiff cock.

Sliding her finger from within Ravens' pliant body, Leigha offers cum covered fingers to Damon's mouth. Opening his lips, Damon stares into Leigha's eyes, transfixed with raw desire. Placing her fingertips between Damon's lips, Leigha watches as his lips close around her fingers with complete trust and gentleness of a soft obedient mouth.

The feeling of excitement she never thought she could experience. Or will ever get to experience it again.

Smiling gently, Leigha feels his tongue tease the tip of her finger, slowly moving her hand forward into his mouth, he sucks Raven's juices from Leigha's finger. Slipping her fingers slowly from his mouth, Leigha casually and possessively traces a tender caress against Damon's chest as Raven gently rocks against his pelvis.

Watching her body move fluidly against his, Leigha notes the expressions on the faces, the pleasure, the longing. Watching Raven move her body in rhythm, Leigha smiles her face contorting in pleasure.

"Please, Mistress, would it please you for this slut to cum?"

Reaching up, Leigha softly caresses Raven's hip nodding her approval. The gasp quiet moan satisfy Leigha with the knowledge of the girl's completion, sliding her hand between their bodies, she feels the wet, warm liquid of Ravens' juices coating Damon's cock.

Playing gently with Raven's labia, her body bucks against Leigha's gentle assault. Damon's growl pushes Leigha to play even more. Accepting the torment, Raven gasps with each twitch of Leigha's fingertip against the hardened nub of the clit. The subtle movement brings Damon ever closer to his own climax.

The growled tones of Damon's desire begin to fill the room, as Leigha continues her torment of Raven, the girl now begging for the torture to end.

"Please Mistress, please don't torment me."

The low growling plea from Damon falls on deaf ears as Leigha's fingers continue to administer pure pleasurable torture on Ravens' soaking cunt, causing her body to convulse against Damon's hips.

"Tell your Mistress when you are about to climax, boy slut. I want to know when you are on the edge."

Still playing with Raven's cunt, Leigha moves her fingers further down the slick slit of Raven's pussy, until her finger slides easily into her vagina, tightening the skin hugging Damon's cock. Rubbing against the suddenly tightened hole, his moan, and clenched fists alert Leigha to his quickening eruption.

Withdrawing her fingers from inside Raven's still convulsing vagina, Leigha indicates for her to dismount Damon's lap, covering his cock with her mouth, she can taste the salty cum covering his throbbing rod. Sucking his cock clean, she fondles his balls, feeling them tighten against his impending climax.

Touching the furry base of Damon's groin with her nose, Leigha hears him beg for his release. Rocking his hips into her mouth, she tastes the first hints of his climax, pulling off his cock, Leigha pumps his rod with her hand until his animalistic growl explodes from his throat.

Pumping his cock in her soft hand, Leigha tightens her grip until Damon's throbbing explosion covers her hand with hot, creamy sperm. Feeling the liquid heat of his seed flow over her hand, Leigha milks his cock until the flesh slowly softens in her grip.

Having had Raven undo Damon's bonds, Leigha rises to watch him work the stiffness out of his arms. As Raven assumes the "Tower" position, kneeling next to the large bed on closed bended knee, thighs touching, head down with eyes cast downward and palm resting quietly turned upward as her fingers fold softly inward toward the palms, Leigha silently waits for Damon to kneel before her in submission.

Watching Damon warily, Leigha narrows her eyes in silent judgment to gauge his body language. As he moves slowly from the large bed, he seems different, less arrogant perhaps, maybe humbled?

Rubbing his wrists in his palms, Damon stands before Leigha, his eyes dark and foreboding. Dropping his head, he slowly kneels before Leigha, in silent submission. With Damon kneeling before her, Leigha rests her hand against the top of his bowed head, softly murmuring his love for her, smiling as tears fill her eyes, she bends slightly to kiss the top of his head and returns her love in softly spoken tones.

www.ingramcontent.com/pod-product-compliance
Lightning Source LLC
LaVergne TN
LVHW091536070526
838199LV00001B/95